DATE DUE

IT'S FUNNY WHERE BEN'S TRAIN TAKES HIM

story by **Robert Burleigh**

pictures by **Joanna Yardley**

ORCHARD BOOKS • NEW YORK

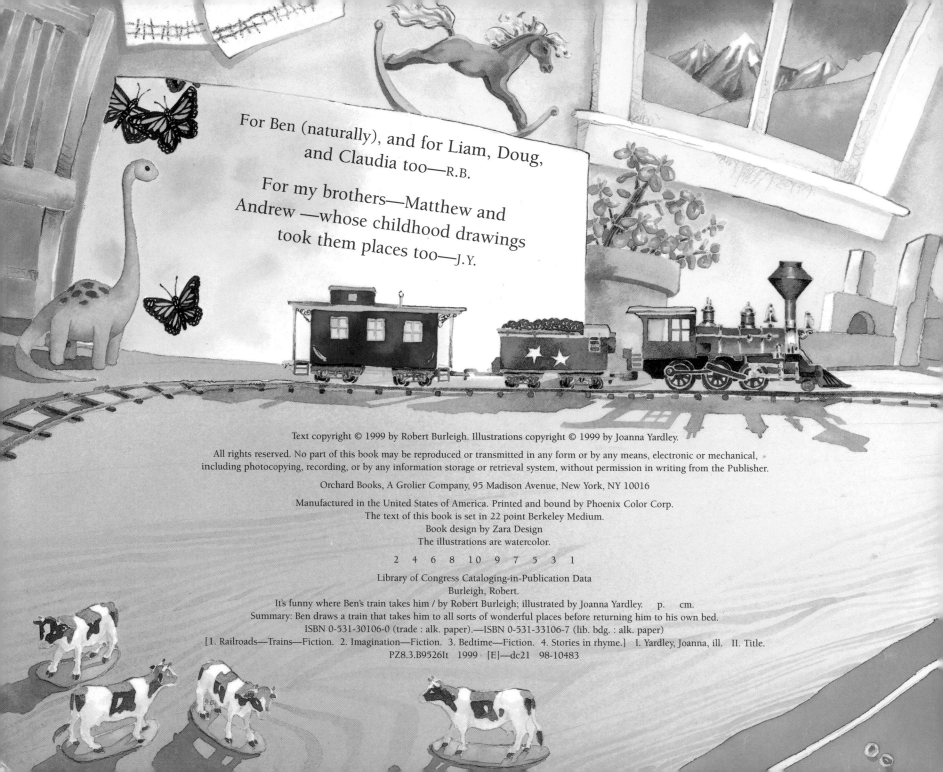

For Ben (naturally), and for Liam, Doug,
and Claudia too—R.B.

For my brothers—Matthew and
Andrew —whose childhood drawings
took them places too—J.Y.

Text copyright © 1999 by Robert Burleigh. Illustrations copyright © 1999 by Joanna Yardley.

Orchard Books, A Grolier Company, 95 Madison Avenue, New York, NY 10016

Manufactured in the United States of America. Printed and bound by Phoenix Color Corp.
The text of this book is set in 22 point Berkeley Medium.
Book design by Zara Design
The illustrations are watercolor.

2 4 6 8 10 9 7 5 3 1

Library of Congress Cataloging-in-Publication Data
Burleigh, Robert.
It's funny where Ben's train takes him / by Robert Burleigh; illustrated by Joanna Yardley.   p.   cm.
Summary: Ben draws a train that takes him to all sorts of wonderful places before returning him to his own bed.
ISBN 0-531-30106-0 (trade : alk. paper).—ISBN 0-531-33106-7 (lib. bdg. : alk. paper)
[1. Railroads—Trains—Fiction. 2. Imagination—Fiction. 3. Bedtime—Fiction. 4. Stories in rhyme.] I. Yardley, Joanna, ill. II. Title.
PZ8.3.B9526It 1999 [E]—dc21 98-10483

Ben draws a train,
With cars and a track.

And sometimes
A caboose in back.

Ben draws a train,
And gets inside!

And then Ben takes
A magical ride.
It's funny where Ben's train takes him.

All aboard!
Train's leaving the shed.

(An engineer's cap
On Ben's head.)

Thick trees wave back.
Tall poles jog by.

Far up ahead's
The distant sky.
It's funny where Ben's train takes him.

Past green hills
Where horses browse,

An old farmhouse,
A field of cows.

And a whir and a whistle
That seem to be saying,

To go *anywhere*
Is better than staying.
It's funny where Ben's train takes him.

A mountain peak
With snow, and then—

Into the dark,
And out again.

Against the window,
Ben presses his nose,

And gazes way down
Where a wide river flows.
It's funny where Ben's train takes him.

Clang! Clang! Clang! Clang!
A little town.

A red light blinks.
A gate goes down.

The city rises.
Ben stares in wonder

At the great glassy buildings
The tracks curve under.
It's funny where Ben's train takes him.

Now through the subway,
And up once more.

Another train passing,
Whoosh and *roar*.

Good-bye! Good-bye!
And then the long light:

Toward the sunset.
Out of sight.
It's funny where Ben's train takes him.

Slow, slow, and slower.
Ben nods his head.

And arrives at the station
Called In-My-Bed.

Where filled with travels,
And train-wheel hums,

He'll dream train dreams
Till morning comes.
It's funny where Ben's train takes him.
It's funny where Ben's train takes him.